Milkman mike
AND THE FIRE ENGINE

GREAT N-ORTHERN

Great Northern Books
PO Box 1380, Bradford, West Yorkshire, BD5 5FB

www.greatnorthernbooks.co.uk

ISBN: 978-1-914227-42-4

Illustrated by Nicky Mills

CIP Data
A catalogue for this book is available from the British Library.

One day **Milkman Mike** was delivering his milk when suddenly he saw something big and red coming down the lane.
It was making a loud noise.
'NEE-NAH-NEE-NAH-NEE-NAH!'
What was it?

"It's a fire engine," said Mike.
"I wonder where it's going?"

The fire engine passed Farmer Cream's cows grazing in the field.

Mike saw Farmer Cream scratching his head.

Farmer Cream also wondered where the fire engine was going.

The fire engine passed Miss Goodness's bakery, where she was making her lemon curds.

Miss Goodness had come out of her shop and was scratching her head too.

Where was the fire engine going? Was there a fire?

Milkman Mike stopped delivering his milk and followed the fire engine in his pickup called Gold Top 2.

Mike waved at Farmer Cream and Miss Goodness as he passed by.

"The fire engine is stopping," said Mike. "I'll go and see if anyone needs help."

When Milkman Mike arrived all he saw was
the fire engine, the firemen and a tree!

"What's going on?" said Mike.

"Would you believe it? There's a big daft dog stuck up in the tree!" said the chief fireman, scratching his head. "I've heard of cats getting stuck in trees, but never a big daft dog!"

"A big daft dog?" said Mike. "Oh no!"

How many big daft dogs did Milkman Mike know?

Only one. Spike!

"A nest?" said Milkman Mike.

"A nest?" said Farmer Cream,
who had followed Mike.

"A nest?" said Miss Goodness,
who had followed Farmer Cream.

"A nest," said the chief fireman.

"Oh no!" said Mike, covering his eyes. "It's Spike!"

"Spike?" said the chief fireman.

"Yes," said Mike. "My big daft dog. I told him not to chase after birds, so he has gone to wait for them to come back instead."

"Spike!" shouted Mike.

"Arr, arr, arr," barked Spike.

"Get down, you big daft dog!" said Mike.

"Arr, arr, arr – arrrrrrr!"
said Spike, and he jumped into
the chief fireman's arms.

"Thank the fireman for catching you, Spike," said Milkman Mike.

Spike licked the chief fireman, on his nose!

"I'm sorry," said Mike. "Thanks for saving him. Have a bottle of milk to make cups of tea for all your firemen."

"And have some of my lemon curds," said Miss Goodness.

"Oh, thanks," said the chief fireman. "That will do nicely for our morning break. And no more going up into trees, Spike, you big daft dog!"

"Arr, arr, arr!" said Spike, and he saluted the chief fireman.

"And no more chasing birds or climbing trees,"
said Farmer Cream.

"Come on, Spike!" said Mike.
"We have more milk to deliver, before I give it all away!"

Also available in the Milkman Mike series

Milkman Mike and the Runaway Bottles

Milkman Mike and the Spaceship

Milkman Mike and the Football Match

www.greatnorthernbooks.co.uk